ZENON Girl of the 21st #1

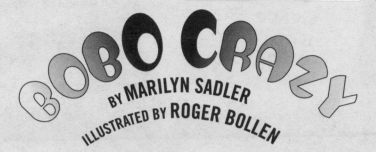

BOBO CRAZY

BY MARILYN SADLER
ILLUSTRATED BY ROGER BOLLEN

Me Bobo.

A Stepping Stone Book™

Random House 🏠 New York

CONTENTS

1
TOBO CRAZY

"But, Mr. Peres, it's *Friday!*" I groaned. "You can't give us homework on *Friday!*"

It was September 24 in the year 2049.

I was in my fifth year of school at Quantum Elementary. I thought that I, Zenon Kar, had seen it all. But homework on Friday was a new one.

"My weekends are important to me, Mr. Peres," I tried again. "I wouldn't give them up for all the stardust in the galaxy!"

Sometimes I wished my parents had never left Earth. The kids say schools down there are easier. But my parents wanted to work in space. So they packed up our ZK4 Space Shuttle and moved to Space Station 9 the year I was born.

There are lots of great things about living on a space station. School just isn't one of them. By the end of the week, I needed to cool my boosters.

My teacher, Mr. Peres, did not see it that way.

"I want your data pad reports on my desk first thing Monday morning" was all he said.

My best friend, Nebula, and I decided to head to the Mars Malt after school. It was the most thermo chill chamber in our sector. And I was pretty sure that a Whambama Shake would ice us out.

When we got to the malt shop, some of

our friends were already there. So we bought our shakes and sat down. It seemed I wasn't the only one flared-up over homework.

"I had big plans this weekend," complained Tad. "Guess I'll have to scrub my mission."

"Me too," said Var.

My poor friends. You become close when you live together on a space station. So if your friends go supernova, you do, too.

I needed another shake.

"Do you want one?" I asked Nebula. Nebula did not answer.

"Ceedus-Lupeedus!" she cried instead.

You're probably thinking that Neb saw something creepy crawling across the wall. But she didn't. We have our own way of talking on Space Station 9. And "Ceedus-Lupeedus" is what we say when we're surprised.

So we all spun around to see why Neb was so inked-out.

On the large 3-D TV was the most stellar robotic flying dog we had ever seen!

"Make no bones about it," a space station newscaster was saying. "Tobomania is sweeping the galaxy. Boys and girls are buying the Tobo Robotic Dogs off the shelves of toy stores everywhere!"

My friends and I could not take our eyes off the TV. Real pets were not allowed on space stations. So the idea of a pet—even a robotic one—was thermo.

We watched in silence as the Tobo Dog flew around the newsroom. After a loop-the-loop and a power dive, it sat down for an interview.

"We can do *so* much more than real dogs can do," bragged the Tobo Dog. "We can fly. We can talk. We can even do homework."

That was all we had to hear.

"I'm getting a Tobo Dog!" said Tad, jumping out of his seat.

"Me too!" said Var.

"Me too!" said Neb.

Then my friends looked at me.

"Don't you want one, Zee?" they all asked.

What could I say? They didn't know my dad.

2
NO, NO, BOBO

I was waiting for my dad when he got home that night.

"You're late," I told him.

My dad did not have to say anything. His hot-pink stress reducer said it all. He was having Fuddle-Frisson problems at work.

I was worried. I wanted him to take me to Z-mart to buy a Tobo Dog.

"Do you want a Fizzy Nasal?" I asked him.

It was his favorite soft drink. The purple bubbles made him sneeze. And sneezing made him happy.

I poured my dad a tall glass of the purple liquid.

"Thank you, honey," he said from inside his stress reducer. After a few swallows, he began to sneeze.

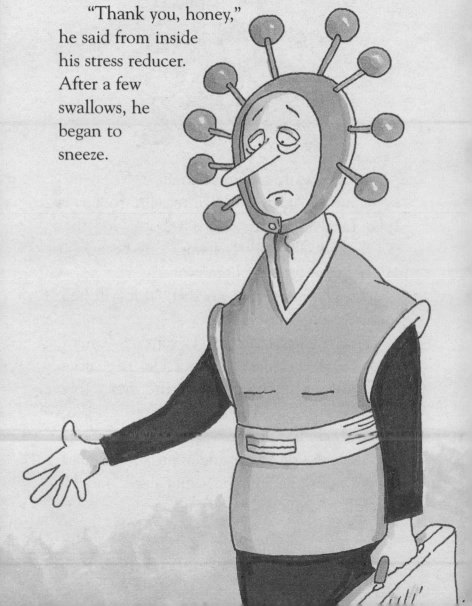

I didn't waste any more time.

"Can we go to Z-mart tonight to buy a Tobo Dog?" I asked. "It's a robotic dog that can fly and talk. Mostly I want one because it will help me with my homework."

"I suppose so," said my dad, "if it will help you in schoo—*ahh-choooo!*"

That night, Dad and I went to Z-mart. There was a large line outside the store. Everyone was talking about the new Tobo Dog.

My dad did not like waiting in lines. So he left me standing there and went into Z-mart. A few minutes later, he came back out. He was still wearing his stress reducer.

"Do you have any idea how much this Tobo Dog costs?" he asked me.

It had not crossed my mind.

"No, Dad," I said. "Is there a problem?"

"They want thirty frackles for that dog!" he fussed.

Slam, I thought. *I should have brought Mom.*

"But, Dad," I started to say. "He flies and he—"

"I don't care if he does loop-the-loops and power dives," he snapped. "I am *not* paying thirty frackles for a hunk of Zarkon metal!"

I did not know what to do. My dad was
going into global meltdown. And the people
in line were staring at us.

"Let's just forget it," I said.

But Dad did not give up easily.

"Let's see if they have anything cheaper,"
he said, walking away from me.

I followed him into Z-mart, feeling
like a Blotozoid Zombie . . . pale . . . shoulders
slumped forward . . . no feeling in my legs.

Then, all of a sudden, Dad stopped at a
display table.

"Look at this!" he said, handing me something yellow and fuzzy. "It's a robotic dog! And it's only *five* frackles!"

It was the dumbest-looking robotic dog I had ever seen. It didn't have ears. It didn't have a mouth. It didn't even have a tail.

"That's not a Tobo," I told my dad. "That's a *Bobo*. And it's junk," I said, tossing it back down on the table.

When I looked up, my dad was already walking toward a salesclerk with a Bobo in his hands.

"No, Dad! I don't want that Bobo!" I shouted at him.

He looked at me in disbelief.

"Either you'll take this dog or you'll get no dog at all!" was his final order.

I was being swallowed up by a black hole right there in Z-mart.

"Buy the stupid dog, then," I said.

The salesclerk took the Bobo Dog from my father. She slipped a battery pack into its head.

It opened its eyes and said, "Me Bobo."

I blasted out of Z-mart as fast as I could. If I lived to be two hundred, I would never understand my dad!

3
NEBULA

The next morning, I woke up in an inky mood. At first, I didn't know why. Then I rolled over and saw the Bobo Dog. It was staring at me.

I bolted out of bed and slammed my bathroom door.

"Ah shwould neber leb ma dab buy em!" I grumbled as I brushed my teeth.

When I came out of the bathroom, the Bobo Dog was waiting for me. It followed me around my room when I got dressed. Then it followed me downstairs to breakfast.

"Morning glorious!" said Woma 2000. She was our robotic maid. Mom couldn't live without her. I couldn't, either.

"What is *this?*" she asked, seeing Bobo for the first time.

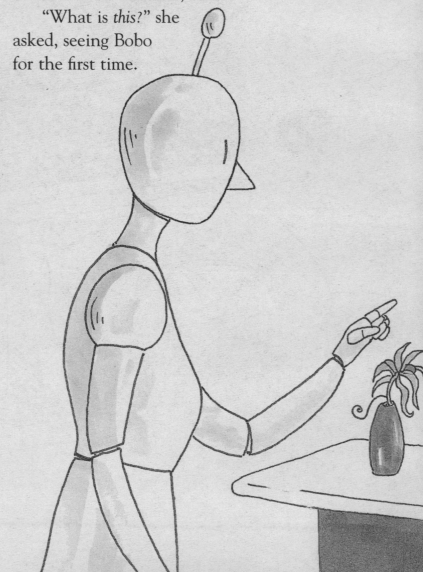

"It's my new robotic dog," I said with a frown. "Dad wouldn't buy me a Tobo. They were too expensive."

"Oh, dear," said Woma. She studied Bobo for a moment.

Then she asked, "Will he be eating anything?"

"No," I said. "He doesn't have a mouth."

Woma fixed me a bowl of Snackle Frax. Then she left the room. Bobo hovered a few feet away, watching me eat.

The door buzzer buzzed, and Woma came back into the kitchen with my best friend, Nebula.

Nebula had on a new Nan Kloddy outfit. Her mother bought her everything she wanted at Saturn Fifth Avenue. And unlike my dad, *her* father never said anything about frackles.

"Hi, Neb," I said.

"Hi, Zee," she said.

Nebula was carrying a big package. She put it on the table. Then she sat down. She waited for me to ask her what was in it. I waited for her to tell me.

Finally, she said, "Guess what I got."

Sometimes Neb fully shivered me out. She always got everything I wanted. She had a 3-D maxi-phone. She had a ten-speed hoverboard. She even had backstage passes to the Microbe concert. And now she probably had something else I wanted.

The minute I had that thought, I got that inky feeling again.

All of a sudden, I wished Nebula hadn't come to visit. I wished she and her big package would just disappear.

"You're not going to believe this, Zee," she said as she opened her box. "But I just got the new Tobo Dog!"

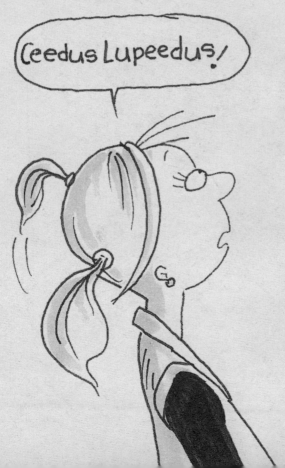

Ceedus Lupeedus!

Ceedus-Lupeedus! Out of the box soared the most stellar Tobo Dog I had ever seen.

4
A ONE-DOG SHOW

The Tobo Dog looked at me. Then it took off and circled the living room. It did a loop-the-loop and a power dive. It looked just like the Tobo on TV.

After it flew around the living room for what seemed like hours, Nebula said, "Let's go to the Big Wheel."

The Big Wheel was our space station shopping mall. Nebula went there *at least* once a day.

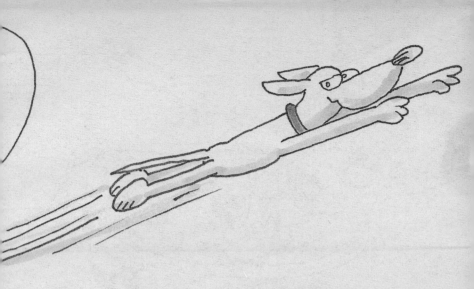

"Not today," I said.

"Then when?" asked Neb. She did not give up easily.

"I don't know," I said. "Later."

"How *much* later?" asked Neb.

Just then my Bobo Dog flew into the room. I didn't want Nebula to see him. So I decided to change my mind.

"How about now?" I said, hurrying her out of our apartment.

Nebula and I got on our hoverboards and cruised down the halls of the space station toward the Big Wheel. The Tobo Dog flew behind us, in front of us, and in circles all around us.

What a show-off, I thought.

When we got to the mall, Neb touched down in every store.

"Tobo will look great in this!" she said, holding up a Zarkon dog collar. "And look! A matching necklace for me!"

Six stores and twelve packages later, we found our friends. They were eating burgers at the McWheel. Their new Tobo Dogs were hovering around them.

"Neb!" Var shouted. "You got a Tobo Dog, too!"

Everyone stopped eating and admired Neb's new Tobo Dog.

"Show them what you can do, Tobo!" said Nebula.

Neb's Tobo took off and flew through the air. He circled the mall high above the shoppers. He dipped and dived. He did the loop-the-loop. He even did his thermo power dive.

Then, as if that weren't enough, he told a few jokes.

"When do dogs have eight legs?" he asked.

"I don't know!" said Tad.

"When there are two of them!" Tobo answered. "What has floppy ears and a tail that goes up and down?"

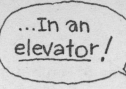

"I don't know!" said Var.

"A dog in an *elevator!*" Tobo answered.

What a scorch.

I'd never seen anything like it. A large crowd had gathered. Everyone was laughing.

The next thing I knew, the dog had the crowd singing.

"Three good dogs, three good dogs, see how they fly, see how they fly...." Their voices echoed throughout the space station.

I was ready to scrub this mission. A little bit of Tobo went a long way. Then, all of a sudden, everyone started laughing again. This time, Tobo was laughing, too.

I swung around to see what was so funny. What I saw fully shivered me out.

My Bobo had come to the shopping mall. And he was floating my way!

5
BAD BOBO

"What's that, Zee?" shrieked Nebula.

"Me Bobo," said Bobo.

I grabbed Bobo, slapped him on the back of my hoverboard, and took off.

"Don't ever follow me like that again!" I scolded him.

"Me bad Bobo," he said, hanging his head.

When I got home, I went straight to my room. Boy, was I flared-up! I slammed my door so hard, I set off every computer in the apartment.

"It is four P.M. The temperature is seventy degrees. Beet loaf and mashed potatoes for dinner," the computer voices shouted at me.

Then my maxi-phone started ringing.

It was Tad.

"Hi, Zee!" he said. "Guess what! My Tobo just finished my homework!"

Ceedus-Lupeedus! I thought. *What next?*

"Neb and Var have their homework done, too," he said. "We're going to the Mars Malt. Too bad you don't have a Tobo, Zee."

Tad blasted off and my maxi-phone screen went black.

That night at dinner, I didn't feel much like talking. I ate my beet loaf in silence. Mom and Dad talked about Fuddle-Frisson.

What an inky day it had been. Now it was Saturday night, and I had homework to do.

I finished my dinner and went back to my room. Bobo slipped in behind me before I had a chance to shut the door.

I sat at my desk and stared at my data pad. Then I stared at Bobo. *Is there a chance he can help me?* I wondered.

I wouldn't know unless I tried.

I called up my data pad dictionary. *If I program him with new words,* I thought, *maybe he will be smarter.*

"Repeat after me," I began. "Aardvark."

Bobo stared at me and said nothing.

So I read another word off my data pad. "Abaca."

But still Bobo said nothing.

So I tried, "Abalone, babble, baboon . . ."

Bobo was silent.

"Then how about *bushed!*" I said. "Because that's what I am!"

I got up from my desk and opened the door.

"If you can't help me, then get out of my room!" I shouted, pointing down the hall. Bobo floated slowly past me. I slammed the door behind him, surprising even myself.

A few minutes later, there was a knock at my door. It was my mom. "Zee, is something wrong?" she asked me. "You haven't been yourself today."

She was right. I hadn't been myself. This Tobo thing was driving me into hyperspace.

"I'm sorry, Mom," I said. "It's just that I really wanted a Tobo Dog."

"I know, Zee," she said. "But you have a Bobo, and Bobo isn't all that bad. In fact, he's kind. He's loyal. And he thinks the universe of you!"

Maybe Mom was right. He was kind. And he was stellarly loyal. I began to feel bad.

"Okay," I agreed. "I'll give Bobo a chance."

Mom gave me a kiss and a hug. Then she left my room.

I finished my homework a little after ten o'clock. It wasn't as inky as I thought it would be. And it had taken my mind off Bobo.

Speaking of Bobo, I haven't seen him all evening, I thought. *He's usually hovering right by my side.*

I climbed into bed and turned off my lights. *Maybe I'm being too mean to him,* I decided. *First thing tomorrow, I'll apologize.*

6
TOBO <u>REALLY</u> CRAZY

The next morning, Bobo was not there by my bed when I opened my eyes. I got dressed and hurried downstairs.

Woma was alone in the kitchen.

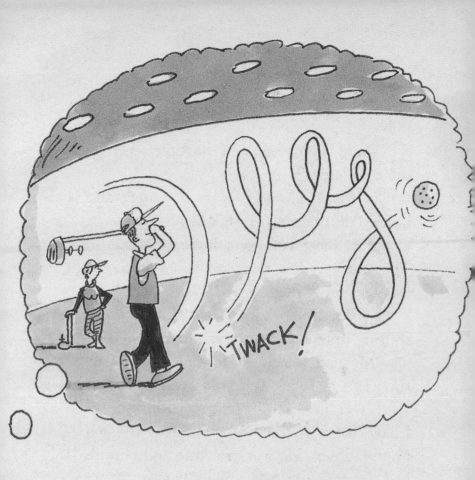

"Where is everyone?" I asked her.

"Your parents went to play a few holes of goofball," she said.

Mom and Dad love to play goofball. It's like the game of golf. Except when you hit the ball, you have no idea where it's going to go.

But I wasn't really wondering where Mom and Dad were. I was wondering about Bobo.

Then Woma said, "I haven't seen Bobo since yesterday."

My maxi-phone began to ring, and I hurried off to answer it. It was Neb.

"Zee, have you gone lunar or something? That fuzzy yellow thing of yours at the mall was a scorch!" she laughed.

I wished Neb hadn't said that. I was just starting to like that fuzzy yellow thing.

"My dad bought it for me," I said. "We thought the Tobos were *way* overpriced."

I was just about to say good-bye when I saw Tobo in the background of the maxi-phone screen. He was growling and barking. I had never seen him act mean before.

"Is he okay, Neb?" I asked.

"Of course he's okay!" she said.

I guess she should know, I thought. Then I hurried off the phone.

I jumped on my hoverboard and flew out the door. I had to find Bobo. I had to tell him I was sorry for being so mean.

I cruised the halls of the space station, stopping at all my usual hangouts. I didn't see Bobo in any of them. But what I did see fully shivered me out.

In the Mars Malt, a Tobo Dog had knocked a Milky Way Float all over the floor.

In the Laser Beam Arcade, a Tobo Dog was fighting with his owner over a game of Micro-Madness.

And in the Mercury Music Store, a Tobo Dog was barking so loud, no one could hear the music.

Everywhere I went, Tobos were growling and barking at everyone.

Then, as I rounded the corner by the Big Wheel, Nebula went tearing by on her hoverboard.

"Ceedus-Lupeedus!" I shouted. "You almost knocked me down!"

To my horror, Nebula's Tobo had his teeth clamped on the seat of her Nan Kloddy jeans. She was screaming and crying.

"Help me, Zee!" she shouted, trying to get away from him. But Tobo was not about to let go!

7
BOBO TO THE RESCUE

I put my hoverboard into gear and took off after Nebula.

Unfortunately, my hoverboard was no match for Neb's Hyperspeed 200. I blasted through the halls of the space station at my highest speed. But Neb disappeared from sight.

I hurried home, hoping that my parents were back from goofball. But when I got there, Woma was alone in the living room. She was watching the news.

"Come see this, Zee!" she shouted. So I turned my attention to our 3-D TV.

"If you are the owner of a Tobo Robotic Dog, please listen carefully," said the newscaster.

"As of today, D.O.G. Industries is recalling its popular robotic dog. The Zarkon metal body frames are causing tuton shorts in their flystroms. As a result, Tobo Dogs are turning mean and are biting their owners!"

(In case you're wondering, a tuton short is some kind of electrical backfire that can happen in things that are robotic. And a flystrom is a small piece of computer equipment found inside every robot. It's part of what makes it work. If you need to know more, you'll have to ask my dad.)

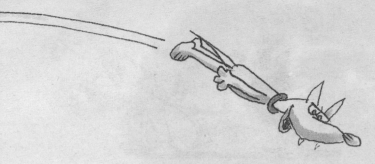

I told Woma everything I had seen that day on the space station. I was just about to tell her about Nebula when my maxi-phone rang.

I hurried to my room and turned on my phone. To my relief, it was Neb!

"My parents aren't home!" she shouted. "Please help me, Zee!"

SNAP!

I could see that Tobo still had ahold of her jeans. He was growling and shaking all over. It was the inkiest thing I had ever seen.

"I'll be right there!" I shouted. Then I jumped on my hoverboard and blasted out of the apartment. I never even had a chance to tell Woma about Nebula.

I flew through the space station.

Mad Tobos were everywhere! They were circling and dive-bombing their owners. They even nipped and growled at *me* as I sped by. When I got to Neb's apartment, the door was already open. So I flew inside. Neb was struggling with her Tobo Dog.

"Oh, Zee! I'm so glad you're here!" she cried.

I grabbed hold of Tobo. I tried to get him away from Nebula. But he had too firm a grip on her Nan Kloddy jeans.

So I tried to reach the controls under his belly. But he was too quick. He wiggled away from me easily.

Then Tobo turned. With his jaws still gripping Nebula's pants, he gave me the meanest look I had ever seen.

From deep in his throat came a low, nasty growl. I took two steps backward and stopped. I didn't know what to do.

Then, all of a sudden, something came flying through the open doorway!

It struck Tobo hard in his side. Tobo went flying across the room. He hit the wall and broke into a hundred pieces!

Nebula and I looked at the pile of Tobo parts on the floor. Then we turned to see what had done this.

To our surprise, something yellow and fuzzy disappeared through the doorway!

8
BOBO GONE

"Bobo . . .," I whispered in awe.

"He saved my life!" shouted Nebula.

Neb and I blasted out of her apartment. We had to find Bobo!

The first place we went was the Big Wheel. There was a huge crowd outside of Z-mart. Everyone was returning Tobo Dogs.

We pushed our way through the crowd. We asked everyone we saw if anyone had seen Bobo.

"He's yellow and fuzzy," said Nebula.

"He doesn't have ears, a mouth, or a tail," I added.

"He sounds stupid," said a boy with green hair, standing in line.

I wanted to punch him. I was so flared-up.

"He may be stupid," I said. "But he's not mean!"

We left the Big Wheel and circled the halls of the 4th Sector.

"Bobooooo!" we shouted.

"What's a Bobo?" someone asked us.

"Only the most thermo dog in the universe!" said Nebula.

Soon it got late, and Neb and I had to go home. Our parents go supernova when we're late.

"We'll look again tomorrow after school," said Nebula, trying to cheer me up.

When I got home, I thought that Bobo might be there. But Bobo was nowhere in sight.

Mom and Dad listened carefully when I told them what had happened.

"Where *is* Bobo?" I cried, throwing my arms around Mom.

"I wab swo mean to hem, Mom," I sobbed. "Pwease com hooom, Bwobwo!"

Then Mom had an idea.

"Let's make some Lost Bobo signs," she said. "We can put them all over the space station."

Mom's idea was thermo. I brightened right up. I got my pens and paper and went to work.

I drew a picture of Bobo at the top of the sign. Then I wrote:

LOST BOBO DOG !

Answers to the name :
"BOBO"
Yellow, fuzzy fur
Very brave - Very strong

Call: Zenon at X25Y99

Dad made a hundred copies of my sign. Then he took me all over the space station. We posted signs in every store, restaurant, and tree park.

By the end of the evening, I was bushed. Dad and I stopped at the Mars Malt on the way home for Whambama Shakes.

"Thanks for helping me with my signs, Dad," I said, giving him a hug. Dad could be pretty thermo sometimes.

When we got home, I went straight to bed. It had been a scorch of a day. But for now, I felt I had done everything I could to find Bobo.

I closed my eyes and fell into a deep sleep. The next morning, I woke up to the sound of my maxi-phone ringing.

9
THE STELLAR STUDENT

I bolted out of bed to answer my phone. I was sure it was someone calling about Bobo.

"May I speak to Zenon?" asked the boy on my maxi-phone screen.

"*I'm* Zenon!" I cried.

"I saw your Bobo Dog sign in the tree park this morning," said the boy.

"You've seen my Bobo Dog?" I shouted.

"Well, no. That's why I was calling," he said. "I was hoping I *could* see him. I want to buy him."

"But I don't have Bobo anymore!" I cried. "He ran away from home!"

"Oh," said the boy. "I thought you were selling him. I read your sign wrong."

The boy turned off his phone, and my screen went black.

What a way to start the day.

I packed up my homework and left for school.

The halls of the space station were quiet that morning. The only sound I heard was the soft hum of my hoverboard.

When I got to school, my friends were waiting for me.

"Sorry about your Bobo Dog," said Tad.

"What a thermo dog he must have been!" said Var.

"Yeah, he was pretty thermo," I said, hanging my head. Neb must have told them about Bobo. No one was laughing now.

The school bell rang, and we hurried to class. Mr. Peres seemed happy to see us.

"Please put your homework on my desk," he said.

We stacked our data pad reports on his desk. Then we sat down.

Mr. Peres talked about macro-bionics that morning—or was it micro-bionics? I guess I wasn't paying attention. My mind was in a Martian mist.

Finally, it was time for lunch. I followed my friends to the lunchroom.

"Guess what, Zee!" said Nebula. "My mom is taking me to Saturn Fifth Avenue tonight to buy a Bobo Dog!"

What little appetite I had was now gone.

"That's great, Neb," I said, trying to look happy.

I was more than ready to go back to class when the bell rang.

"I graded your homework during lunch," Mr. Peres began as we sat down at our desks. "And I must say, I am very disappointed in almost all of you."

Mr. Peres walked around the room, handing back our data pad reports. We sat quietly, waiting for the next comet to fall from the sky.

"It is very clear to me that you all used the Tobo Robotic Dog to do your homework reports," he said. "Every one of them reads *exactly* the same! Therefore, I have no choice but to flunk this class."

A loud groan rang out from my friends. Then Mr. Peres stopped at my desk.

"Zenon Kar, on the other hand, did not

seek the help of a robotic dog," he said. "It is clear to me that she did her *own* homework. She is the only one who passes!"

Mr. Peres handed me my homework. At the top of my data pad was an A!

"Good work, Zenon," he said. "Keep thinking for yourself."

It had been an inky Monday. But for this one Microbe moment, I was happy.

10
BOBO CRAZY

"Are you all right, Zee?" Mom asked when I got home that night.

The excitement over my good grade had worn off. I'd been swallowed up by a black hole again.

"Not really, Mom." I began to cry. "I miss Bobo."

Dad came over and put his arm around me.

"I have an idea, Zee," he said. "Let's go to Z-mart right now and buy you a *new* Bobo!"

I know my dad meant well. But I didn't want a new Bobo. I wanted the one I had.

Before I could make Dad understand, he pushed me out the door. He took my hand. And he pulled me down the hall of the space station toward the Big Wheel.

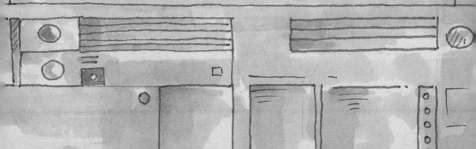

When we got to Z-mart, there was a large crowd outside.

They're probably still returning Tobo Dogs, I thought. But to my surprise, they were buying Bobos!

Ceedus-Lupeedus!

Dad and I followed the line into the store. We listened while everyone talked about the Bobo Dog.

"Bobo is so cute without ears, a mouth, or a tail!" one girl said.

"The Bobo is very strong and brave, too," said a boy.

Finally, Dad and I made our way into Z-mart. In the front of the store was a large display of Bobos. The sign above them read NEW & IMPROVED BOBO ROBOTIC DOG.

How have the Bobos been improved? I wondered. They looked the same to me.

"The only difference I can see," said Dad, "is the price!"

Dad was right. The new Bobo was now *forty-four* frackles! It was even more expensive than the Tobo Dog had been!

I walked around the store while Dad put on his stress reducer.

He probably won't buy a Bobo now, I thought. And that was fine with me.

Then something caught my eye and I stopped walking.

There was a Bobo sitting all alone on a table. It had a sale tag on it that read 50% OFF.

Why is this Bobo so cheap? I wondered.

I walked over to look at it.

When the Bobo saw me coming, it floated up from the table and over toward me. It looked very excited.

Then it said, "Me Bobo!"

Ceedus-Lupeedus! I could not believe my eyes! It was *my* Bobo!

11
BOBO HOME

"Bobo!" I cried. "I've found you at last!"

I picked up Bobo and hugged him so hard, I almost bent his Zarkon metal body frame.

"I will never be mean to you again!" I promised.

I was so excited, I ran over to Dad. He was still standing in line.

"Look, Dad!" I shouted. "It's Bobo! He was over there on the *previously owned* table!"

I can always tell when my dad is happy. And at that moment, he was very happy. Not only had I found Bobo, but Bobo was *on sale*.

"It's good to see you, Bobo," he said, rubbing Bobo's fuzzy yellow head. "We really missed you."

Then, all of a sudden, Dad's face got inky.

"Hold on a moment," he said, thinking carefully.

"I already *bought* this Bobo once."

Dad turned to the salesclerk and held Bobo up for him to see.

"I bought this Bobo Dog on Friday," he said. "I'm not about to buy him again today."

"I'm sorry, sir, but you must not have read the instructions on his tag," said the salesclerk. "It reads: *'If your Bobo is not wanted, it will return to the store. You will not be given a refund.'* You must not have wanted this Bobo, sir."

Dad looked at me. I looked at the salesclerk. He was right. The Bobo had not been wanted. But now the Bobo was wanted more than anything. And I wasn't about to lose him.

"*I'll* buy him, Dad!" I shouted.

Dad looked at me with surprise. Then he put his hand on my shoulder and smiled.

"That's a very good idea, honey," he said.

I reached into my pocket and pulled out twenty-two frackles (Bobo's markdown price). It was all I had. But it was a small price to pay for Bobo.

The salesclerk handed me Bobo, and we hurried out of the store. I couldn't wait to get home.

"Look who we found!" I shouted as I burst
into the apartment.

Mom and Woma were sitting in the
kitchen. They couldn't believe we had found
Bobo. They hugged and kissed him and made
a big fuss.

"It wasn't the same around here without
you, Bobo!" said Woma.

Mom had to agree.

Then the door buzzer buzzed and Woma
went to answer it. She came back into the
kitchen with Nebula.

"I wanted you to see my new Bobo Dog!"
said Neb. She stepped aside to let him pass by.

"He looks great, Neb!" I said, smiling.

Then Nebula spotted Bobo floating next
to me.

"You've found Bobo!" she cried, running over to him. Neb hugged Bobo for a long time. Then she hugged me.

It was so thermo. It was a real Microbe moment.

I could tell that Neb was happy. You become close when you live on a space station together. So if your friends are happy, you are, too. That's pretty much how it is on Space Station 9. It's one of the things I like best.

12
ZENON'S GUIDE TO SPACE STATION SLANG

These are some of the terms you'll hear when you visit me on Space Station 9:

Big Wheel

We call our space station the Big Wheel. It looks like a big wheel floating in outer space! It is also the name of our shopping mall. I think they should change the name

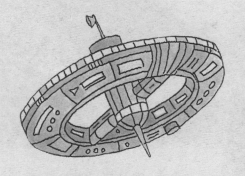

to Nebula, though. That's my best friend's name. She spends more time and frackles there than anyone.

Blotozoid Zombie

This is a character from one of the scariest movies I have ever seen, *The Night of the Blotozoid Zombies!* A Blotozoid Zombie is very pale, and it slumps forward when it walks. Yuck!

Ceedus-Lupeedus!
This is our favorite thing to say when we are surprised by something we see or hear.

chill chamber
This is a place, like the Mars Malt, where we go to relax.

cool your boosters
This means you need to calm down and take it easy. I have a hard time with this one.

data pads
These are our portable computers. My friends and I take them everywhere with us. We carry them in our backpacks.

flared-up
You're flared-up when you're upset and angry. Sometimes your face can turn as red as a solar flare, too.

flystrom
You will find this small piece of computer equipment inside every robot. It's part of what makes it work. If you need to know more, you'll have to ask my dad.

frackles
This is what we call our money. Dad has a hard time parting with his.

Fuddle-Frisson
This is the name of the big project my dad has been working on since we came to the space station. What it is exactly, I don't have a clue.

global meltdown
This happens when you get upset and lose control of yourself.

goofball

Mom and Dad love to play goofball. It's like the game of golf, except that when you hit the ball, you have no idea where it's going to go.

hoverboard

My friends and I go everywhere on our hoverboards! They look like skateboards, except they hover above the ground and fly.

hyperspace

(as in "drive you into hyperspace")

This is when someone is driving you crazy. For example, my dad and my teacher, Mr. Peres, can drive me into hyperspace.

ice out

If you need to ice out, it means you need to relax and calm down. Going to a chill chamber, like the Mars Malt, can help.

inked-out or **inky**
This is when you're spooked or scared or when something really gives you the creeps.

lunar
(as in "going lunar")
This is the same as going crazy.

macro-bionics
This is the study of big robots.

Martian mist
When your mind is kind of foggy and confused, you're in a Martian mist.

maxi-phone
I love my maxi-phone! It has a large screen so I can see my friends when I'm talking to them.

Microbe
This is the name of my favorite rock group. The lead singer, Proto Zoa, is out of this world!

Microbe moment
This is a really wonderful moment in time. Seeing Microbe in concert would be a Microbe moment for sure.

micro-bionics
This is the study of small robots, like Bobo.

Nan Kloddy
She is the space station's favorite, but expensive, clothing designer. My best friend, Nebula, has *all* her clothes. I have *one* pair of her jeans.

scorch
When something is a scorch, it's a bad, bad thing.

scrub a mission

This is when you give up what you are doing and move on to something else.

shivered me out

You get this way when something or someone really gives you the creeps.

slam

This is what we say when we're upset about something. It comes from getting angry and slamming a door.

stellar

If something is stellar, it is the most wonderful thing you can imagine!

stress reducer
This is a helmet you put on your head when you need help in calming down. My dad practically lives in his.

supernova
(as in "going supernova")
If you go supernova, you become very upset. It's kind of like going into global meltdown.

swallowed up by a black hole
You can feel like you've been swallowed up by a black hole when you feel really bad about something.

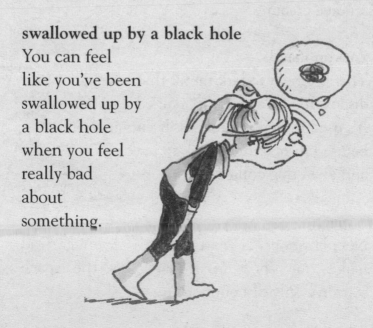

thermo
This is something hot, hip, and stellarly cool!

tuton short
This is an electrical backfire
that can happen in things
that are robotic.

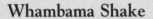

Whambama Shake
No one loves this milkshake more
than I do! It's made from whambama berries
and ice cream.

Zarkon metal
This is a heavy, dark metal that was
discovered by a scientist named Zarkon.
It's used in making robots. It can also
be used in making clothing, jewelry,
and even dog collars.

BUD ZARCON

Z-mart
Nebula shops at Saturn Fifth Avenue. Dad
makes me shop at Z-mart. It's the space
station's only discount store.

ABOUT THE CREATORS

MARILYN SADLER and **ROGER BOLLEN** have been creating children's books for over twenty years. Their best-selling titles include the Alistair series of books and the P. J. Funnybunny books, published as Beginner Books by Random House. Their many awards include the International Reading Association Classroom Choice Award and a *Parents' Choice* Award.

Marilyn and Roger originally created Zenon for a hardcover picture book. Then, in January 1999, Disney Channel produced *Zenon, Girl of the 21st Century* as a ninety-minute live-action film. It became the #1 most popular original television movie that year for the channel. This has led Disney to create a second Zenon television movie, which will air in 2001.